You
And
Me
Darling

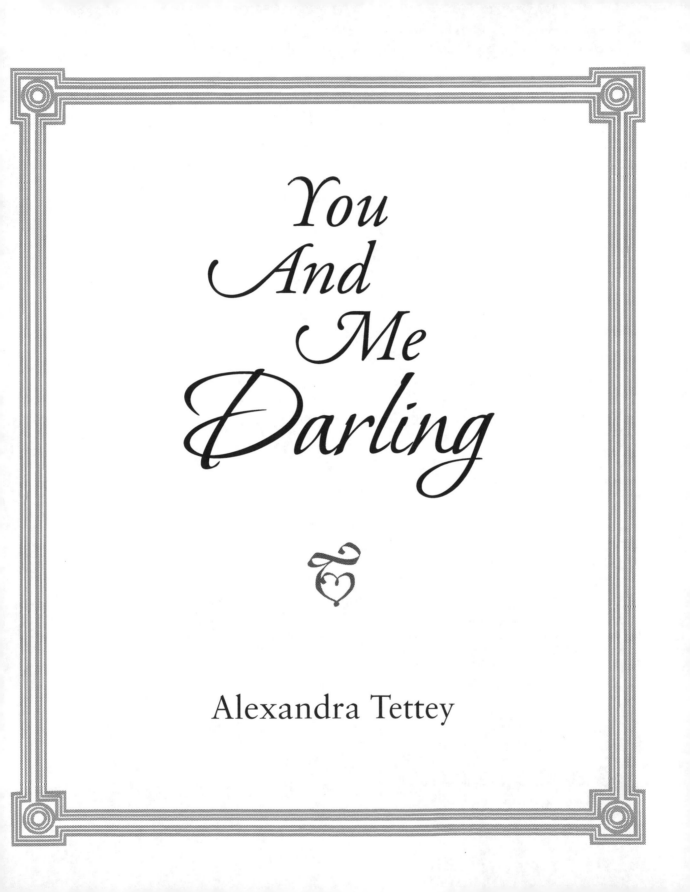

Alexandra Tettey

Order this book online at www.trafford.com
or email orders@trafford.com

Most Trafford titles are also available at major online book retailers.

Printed in the United States of America.

ISBN: 978-1-4669-7962-8 (sc)
ISBN: 978-1-4669-7963-5 (e)

Trafford rev. 03/01/2013

 www.trafford.com

North America & international
toll-free: 1 888 232 4444 (USA & Canada)
phone: 250 383 6864 ♦ fax: 812 355 4082

Contents

Terrible War

The war was hard

I dodged every bullet that shot against me

That was in 1952 against brutal Germany

their eyes were fading us bit by bit gradually

Like poison reacting through us maliciously.

We were taught to have no fear

but fear clearly meant we were alive.

I will not let their weapons strike me,

I new A I would have lost

And the unending hope England had would seize away

Because I was there optimism

I made them smile endlessly

when they felt there was no more England

And laid in the dirt looking dead like a captured bird

pronounced dead on the land

That was sad

They didn't believe that we would win

But when I saw my only companion

get swept away by the power of the Germans.

I died inside.

My emotions seeped deep down within me

like a dripping heart full of damage.

Unexpectedly the air blew gushes of dust in my eye

travelling at an unbelievable distance

I couldn't see in one eye

They were firing at me constantly but they missed

1978 was worse we went to war

again with half of them dead

I buried my pain, anguish

by manipulating the fact that their

country was in ruins anyway

1978 was such a pity

I died it was not like the others

but undoubtedly more painful the bullet hit the good part

This was more distressing for everyone I left baby D,

Paddy my stepdad and my mother who

couldn't imagine a day without me

and last of all my one and only Pete Doherty Williams

The war slowly began to end magnificently

3 days after my death

If only i was there to see it as that was my wish

Terrible war

Purpose of the story: Is for people in general to feel sympathetic and establish the fact that all the soldiers felt despair. According to the effective words used in the poem. Furthermore this shows these soldiers are upset about leaving there family besides the fact that they feel a surge of happiness and well privileged to fight for their country. On the other they feel fearful of dying and never seeing their families again

Give Up Your Ghost

We gave our salutations, we said our vows

We pledged to them we would love everyone

And despise the forbidden monster leaking through us

We knew exclusively that,

that prevailing spirit was around.

And sometimes lying down like a fellow

of are's beneath our mighty shoe that yarns its yarn

and breathes its weighty breath.

Does not the right path to consider always.

But refuses.

You indict me for such unrighteous acts of existence Battle,

burie may be banish, beat my sole if

it may drift into the lake.

You must recapitulate the purpose of the river

it is to wash your thoughts

like washing your heart out thoroughly with integrity.

With the book that the priest delivered to your door step.

It was for you to articulate

with that commanding spirit

and give up your ghost.

The lake took away your gleeful thoughts

and replaced it with the bad.

Now give up your ghost to the eternal

lover of our homeland.

Then you shall see what comes to you

there is one last chance

but you must divert and

there is one way and

never another you must give up your ghost.

The purpose of this poem is to surrender one's self to god. Specifically for committing the wrong things in life. For instincts the lake is portrayed as the devil in the poem whereby the devil brainwashes a believer of god. Furthermore this enables the devil to precisely control the persons thoughts as well make them stop believing in god. On the other hand. The narrator in the poem is advising the doubter of god to be reborn again by giving up his sole.

Sexy lady

The curves on your body make my mouth dribble

When you fingered your cunt

You let all the birds sing

The handcuffs and the wipes I will buy

them because I know that's what

You like don't you?

Your crys and screams drowned me with

a massive big puddle at night

My lonesome nights are over

And you have finally cum to stay

Sexy lady

Your kisses are paralysis within my legs

I worship you my goddess

And wherever you are is never too far

My sexy lady

You are the one

When you grind your hips and dig your cunt into my pipe

I am unconscious with your superior love

Taste me and wipe me

My desire is yours and no matter

how much you give me your

Love would never be too much

My sexy lady

Don't be cruel to me the only place is my wipes and chains

Ill will shed your blood like water as I

worship you with candle wax

And delirious unison with the beat of my melody

You are never too much my sexy lady

Tender Lady

The Chains and the bondage was getting

to much as I tried to pull

Away his nails dug into my tits and then is saw my slit

My pussy was slit into two

So I did not bother to escape

cos the whole scenery looked like a mascerade

There was people laughing as my pussy gyrated to the beat

"Oh what a tender lady they all would shout

My heart skipped a beat

and then I began to dance around the

room like a possessed lunatic

My nipples were stuck with pins as I

felt a sudden touch pulsate

Through my mould and then I screamed because I felt nails

And hammers going into my ass

"Oh what a tender lady they all began to shout

The circus was crowded again

with thousands of fuckers

And the night began to spurt

and I new I was not a flirt

I screamed and screamed

until the hammers went through my ass

and up my anus and through my

Mouth

And into my south again

"Oh what a tender lady she cannot handle her pony"

They all shouted

Fuck you and fuck your fucker

Cos your such a sucker

Can I have my knickers back

But they still began to shout

Oh what a tender lady she is

Good by my friend

You were the one when I needed you

You were there when I felt like life was over

You were the one when I cared and felt like I was daring

And when I didn't want to be me anymore

You picked me up when I felt like my life had ended

When I new I had nothing you gave me what you had

To make me feel happy again

And when I wanted to dye you helped me to live

Cos what was there to live for

You put the smile back on my face even

though their was nothing to smile about

But i smiled because you wanted me to

You picked me up when I sank deep in my sorrow

You were the one when there was nothing left of me

You helped me find me

My tiny little world

You put it together again

The depression I was battling with took

away that very good part of me

It cut internally and unpleasurably like a sword

Stealing a way the real me

And when you left I dyed inside I don't

think about you leaving me

I appreciate what you did for me and do not depreciate

The help you gave me to carry on with my life

Is nothing that comes close

You were my true friend

Wherever you are now thank you

I wanted to write you a letter to tell you I'm better now

But I don't no if you received it

But all I say is thank you

And farewell my good friend

We swam for our lives

The waves were unfriendly

they howled at us,

as we swam and swam

so hurriedly to wherever

There was no trying to figure out

if we were destined to hurt

IF WE were it was too late

we should have thought this thought before

as they were out to get us and

we didn't prolong our thinking in regards to this

it's that we assumed we had your friendship

but instead you have turned into an irate wave

that wants something from us.

But we have nothing so what is it you want,

leave us alone.

I begin to scurry through the cooling irrigate

and swiftly look back and there is no sight of my friend.

My hands are trembling with anticipation

that they will emerge from the water.

I wait and wait and wait so unwearyingly

but deep inside I no the answer but deny myself.

My only friend has gone

but where I don't no and will he come back

I ask myself so relentlessly.

The wind begins to push me

sending me an intimation of a signal to swim

it speaks to me and touches me

with its solicitous hands.

I swim without delay.

Whilst trying to release all the fear from within me.

I am a fearless creature in the water

and my mission is to get away

but still cynical if it's possible.

My heart burning

like deceased ash from my grandfathers cigar,

nevertheless I still was watchful as an owl.

This thing that possess s amplitude and

longitudinal has turned evil,

swallowed my friend and is now out to get me

so i swim with slight determination

as my body is gradually sinking me

I feel to yield myself to this monstrous energy

but continue to swim oblivious to other hazards

I cannot breathe

the water is choking me

don't care about that as long as I get away.

Then abruptly the night becomes solitaire,

comes to a finale and vanishes,

the wave takes me away into its long lost rhapsody arms.

And here I am the evil wave

The whisperers

We heard whispering coming from the back door

It was nothing because I checked before

It was only a glimpse of mistiness that crept beyond us

Nobody was there

We heard children's voices which

sounded like painful sounds of

Whimpers

It was nothing because I checked before

Although i new their was something peculiar about

The house next door

An old dainty looking house

That stared at you and made you quiver

and as you walked by you would start to

Shiver

I heard whisperers emerging from that house

Yesterday

it was nothing because I heard it before

That night I tucked myself away into my shallow bed i

Did not quiver at all

But suddenly I heard the whispers

which I heard the other night

I stayed at mother's house

The whispers grew close

And I new I was not imagining things

It was the children next door who

crept through my backdoor

I reached out my hand but my hand felt cold

And then the children abruptly disappeared before my eyes

And then I new it was only the whisperers

i ust to no that diared next door

You, you, you

Picking up the pile of rubbish

that flew across the

Road I was still trying to discard the

saddening but reminiscent

Memories that leaked like a puddle throughout my head

I am broken in two and it's hard to explain personally

I know I'm, blunt at times it's just hard two love

You when you know you dream of being that

bad someone one day who hurts and kills

people as if nothing ever happened

When you think about doing that it

utterly burns me. Everything burns

And let me tell you, there was nothing I

was hiding you was the one that was

I undid my love for you many

Years ago if you tell me the truth of what

you did then I might take you back

Own up darling.

Remember when you scolded a village of people

like burning wax and

recited malicious words on placing

the censure on someone you claimed

you loved and that was me.

As the leaves blew horrendously

with little notion you gave.

Suddenly everything evolved around you and only you,

you were selfish in your own secret way

you never gave or thought about others

it was always about you

then you appeared and erupted with such guffaw.

you appeared artful in looks and warm glee

was free from the atmosphere you chose me

to throw the rubbish on

and why because I was good to you and held you

in my arms so securely and made you feel loved

was I a forbidden clanger to you all something.

Up to this day it would always be about

you, you, you

The graveyard enemy
I sympathize

There appeared to me

that there was no sign of dismay

As they walked through the distant grounds

that stole a smile of glory through every nation

discarding the good times.

The atmosphere was full of misery and silent weeps

It was nothing but heartbreak,

whose all I could do was imagine you in the clouds

peering down at me reassuring me t

hat everything will be all right.

occasionally I felt good coming here

but today was different the place

Felt spine-chilling but holy at the same time

we came here to visit our deceased enemy

Though I disliked him

I still felt sympathetic and lost

especially when the trees roared like an angry lion

and the mistiness of the sky seemed unwelcoming

I felt a heaviness emerging out of me

I was alone though I bring them with me.

Throughout my unfair years being mistreated by you

now I watch you in your steep pit.

You hurt me but I still miss you

and think about you momentarily

but not all the time.

You wasn't that special to me

I ought to hold you

and tell you that what I feel is beyond

Misery it's a pain that pores within my veins

and encases my optimism with its bare hands

The presences here won't disregard me will they?

I will not come back if they will

.I'm sorry I feel that way I won't come back here

and oblivious thinking on what I feel

and how I want to characterize you is not determined

yet but I wish to be this way soon

I'm sorry I don't want you leaking in my thoughts

go away please my unholy pal

I love you and I don't.

You are my friend

you are not polluting my dreams

by sticking to me like a bewildering animal

who lacks my attention

graveyard creature you are unfortunate.

Stay away

We get jealous

We don't have a problem with you being

goofy but your far to snooty

We get jealous you see, especially the fella's

Your body cruelly derides us

And you exude a swagger so startling

its breaking are eyes, we hate it

As you strut your sexy stuff along the street your tits

flare up like protruding daggers. We get jealous

When you laugh we depreciate, you smile at us

and give us things, but yet we don't appreciate.

We discreetly think your funny but you laugh like a bunny

When boys come near you you're flirty

and in fact we think it's dirty

The day becomes insensitively dark and you

feel fruity the boys are out of site

You yearn for enthralling attention you don't

get it so you pull down your knickers

In the middle of the hub and begin to manipulate

your pussy in the most pleasurable way

We come over and kick u all over the boy conveys his cock

and we make you suck it as that's what you wanted.

Although were sinister we didn't

make you suck just any cock

And as horny as you are I think you need a fuck

You are the tearing dilemma that makes us go mad

As a matter of fact I think it's rather sad.

You are a flourishing, flower

When people here your melodic voice purifying

the air, they stop and stare, it's not fair

The power you behold is a killer

And that why were jealous

Will you make love to me?

The glistening of your body against mine is magnificent

The beauty you hold I cannot deny

You touch my body and I begin to rise high into

another place where it's just me and you

If I cannot hold you I want you inside me

feeling my erotica imagination

Explode without a fight; I came here

to induce you to love me

I to pretend I'm with you everyday

And it's not a case of if you will make love to me

You have too

Because ill hurt you if you don't

Please

Touch me

Hold me

Kiss me

And rumble and caress my divine innocence

It's not a case of if you will touch me

I know you will

You told me you would in my dreams

Will you make love to me?

Cos I love you so much I'm paralysed

Hold me tight and sex me all night until

the day has died without any mystify

Baby please I've been watching you

but I would never tell you that

I believe in you

So believe in me

I stalk you and even walk with you on a hot summer's day

The urge to choke you is overbearing

It's not a case of if you will

I know you will

You need to let me know that you will

Cos I'm not giving up for a kill

Imagining things is not the same it's just a foolish

Lust

You need to get over your self

Because you think you're better than everyone else

Acting the way you act

You think I'm obsessed with you

But it's not a case of if I am

You know I am

And I'm not giving up for the kill

Cos I love you although I've just met you

Will you make love to me?

How I Wish

OH MY, WHEN I FIRST SAW YOU

I Couldn't BELIEVE MY EYE

I NEED YOU,

GOT TO BE YOU with you my precious,

YOUR PHILOSOPHY OF

WHAT YOU DO ENTANGLED ME IN STRINGS

OF GREAT Honour WHY DID I LOVE YOU WHEN I

FIRST SAW YOU

AND WHY DID I LOOSE ALL I HAD

JUST FOR YOU

THE PICTURES,

PAINTINGS,

my affiliation

AND OTHER THINGS I WONT MENTION;

You Took my entire consciousness

with one glance of your beauty

you struck me like fire

I was speechless when you offered me to dance

oh my you are wonderful

I said to my self constantly

with an utter of mourning gladness you said me.

And suddenly I seized your heart

hoping you wouldn't change your mind.

There was no hesitation on what I felt.

I wish you would drown my body with flowers.

my dangerous beauty

let me forget about the bad times

and send me your hot flaming desire of deep

love tell me you will hold me so tight

you will smother my bewildering unexplainable dreams

with love you had for me

i wish you would love me oh my oh

my how i wish you were mine

Your wedding

Brush your hair

Pamper yourself with makeup

so extreme but translucent.

Make each one explode with admiration.

Do your required mundane routine

hat bedazzles People for such reasons. I

Don't understand your confusing beauty

a beauty rebuilt throughout the years

to something remarkably greater than my love.

My love, luscious, lover. Devotee is my command

i will give it to you by surrendering my everything

precisely to your entire requests

to be laid out flat before you and to you.

But not in a worldly of fantasy.

This is real.

Yours.

My love, luscious, lover. Devotee.

So prepare yourself.

There is no need to be shy there all downstairs

You need to make a stand

your being ridiculous my love

you should feel merriment

and wholehearted of this day.

Each one is waiting patiently.

They are not eager.

But they are dying to see your honoured magnificence.

So come down the stairs make your vows to me my lover.

This is your wedding.

The poem is about a woman about to get married to a man. Apparently the woman is less determined to marry this man. Whereby the man is much more eager. He tries to encourage her to be happier by telling her this is actually her big day and not his. On the other hand she feels adamant and also shy to come down the stairs with her wedding dress on and present herself while saying her vows to her branded to be husband to several people. As she feels doubtful of this day.

I wanted to be like you

I loved the way your hair would sway

throughout that torturing wind

swiftly saying you loved me without words

Back then my sweetheart, liar you took my everything

And left me with nothing

But I can't explain how much I still love you

My, my dear darling I wanted to be like you

I wanted to have what you had

And what you desired;

all the things that made you smile,

I wanted what you required deeply and the dearest

I hoped for all the things you wished for

and hope that one day I'll find the spitting courage

to forgive you but at this present moment I am

lost for words, speechless;

like someone who has being struck by

lightning just cannot believe a lot of things.

When you faded away I cried.

My personal imitation

Of you didn't know what to do with its self

Well I'm sorry if my self-centred, snoopy, scrutinizing ways

Had you feeling low a lot of the time.

I wanted to be like you

And that's it was

Changes in you

When they laughed and smiled about the good

Things and banished the worst that created demons

The sad, things like hanging out with long lost alienate

Friends didn't interest us anymore nothing did sometimes

I'd feel lack lustred for no apparent reason,

sad then happy I didn't understand

that taking critics messed with your head

Like ahead rush. I acknowledged the

fact that people come and go

Like when I had dinner with you

and then after the atmosphere had secretly anaesthetized

There I was alone again in that empty house

There was emphasis on silence

only the tapping of my loud shoes

against the tender floor that mum and dad used to possess

Where they lay is prohibited within

time I shall discern my idea

With my dark

Starry-eyed expression that prays for love that

that somebody would one day have for me

The ugly monster

His arms were covered in hair and his dick was humongous

His eyes bulged out at the back of his head

And when he ate he ate with anger and bitterness

As if he was tearing into the skin of a human being

But he bestowed a sensuality and sensuality like no one lese

But that still didn't deny

What such an ugly monster he was

When he laughed he made me sick

And I new if I attacked the beast ill be heading to the nick

Oh what a prick

He was extremely factious he laughed a bitter laugh when
   things went funny

And when I turned around I heard people shouting dummy

But he had the most beautiful pearl drop eyes

I've ever seen before which made my heart stop

And then flick one beat to the next

But that still didn't denied what ugly monster he was

He ate like a beast and I could've sworn he was eating

The old lady's leg next door

The ugly monster

The long walk home

It was a long walk home

Tanya, Fred and Toni all had to walk back

My legs were as swollen as a basketball

I pissed myself on the walk back home

Because we'd all been drinking heavily that night before

From vodka to spirits and tequila to jack daniels

I knew that in this desolate place we had lost our way

And I felt small and deprived because the ones that I
    thought were my friends were

Not

I knew that Tanya loved me it's the way that she looked at me

Her kisses and her presents made me feel a part of them

But the rest of them were deranged

This long journey back wasn't making things easier

We must have took the wrong turning

But it still didn't give it a right for Toni and Fred to jump in
  my bed

But like I said they were small and deranged

And I felt belittled because Tanya sat and watched

And there the wind bellowed drastically and my arms, legs
  and buttocks felt victimised

And then I knew it was going to be a long walk home

Delicious

His hand reached for my skirt

As he moved closer

The touch of his manhood

Urged me to take that deliberate and sensuous action

Of wanting him

He fancied me and I new it

So together he was delicious

He was taking me to another realm which I never new

before

His smile was delicious but his eyes felt like daggers as they

undressed me

He was delicious, delicious he was

He turned the world around with just one touch of it

Everyone new he was mine

That's why they burned whenever he was around

And when his desire could last was no question

For all you know it could last forever

He tasted like honey as I sucked away

And there he was in my arms like I would always see

He was delicious

Erotica

Leather straps and chains are erotic

Wiping and smacking are hypnotic and make you

Feel sexually amused

Candle wax and nipple tazzels make men go wow

Anal beads and romance books are wonderful

And fruits and licking make me feel beautiful

The feel of rubble and painful strikes without the light are

    compulsory

If you cannot handle it do not bother desire for it

Belts and buckles against my skin and leather clothing is so

    startling and I start

to feel like laundering my mind

From such thoughts

No word would ever explain

The beauty of erotica

Material things

All my friend had all moved far away

They left without saying goodbye

And when I called to say hi they would always

Say bye bye

My friends didn't want to know me anymore

As they all drove fancy cars and look down on the others

My friends forgot about me

And never even attended my graduation day

They cared more about the material things

Like hanging in the hot burning sun, chasing stars and

    dishing there money to anything that looked pretty

I feel sorry for them

Cos they are my friends

And will always be my friends

As they never new it would cost them something difficult

They didn't think twice

And they didn't even wonder about the years ahead

And never thought they would die without there dimes but

   the trash in the can

As they cared to much about the material

things

Angels and demons

People come in all shapes and forms you just don't know

who's one of them

Angels and demons are tricky characters next minute there

their next minute there not

They hover and lurk beside you when you think there not

Tell you things subconsciously and stroke your hair in the

gut of the night

Angels and demons

No what they're doing

They watch your sins and write them down

They make a decision whether you belong in heaven or hell

Angels and demons

Act like they are your friends when they only want to

speculate

They creep behind you when you lie they tell you things

others don't which is darkness and light

They wake with us in are shadow when we wake up at

night

Angels and demons

Are not here to cause a fright

They only want us to see the light, not the demon

But the angels

Wants to help us

Angels and demons

Blow me a kiss

Underneath the covers you stroked me in the inside

You pulled me closer, looked into my bedazzled eyes

Then made love to me

It was lovely

And underneath the covers you muttered sweet words

Into my ear like you want to take me there and never look

   back

and I thought

Finally I'm not sleeping alone tonight

Your passion of love making was sweet and as daring as
    could be
You gently pulled my knickers down and left your
    magnificent stains on my neck

That I would never forget
And as the beginning of the day had suddenly perished
You was leaving soon and back to her

Before you left me behind you told me you will come back
But you never did

You always gave me promises but never stuck by them
You gave her nice things and what about me
You never made her have to worry cos she always had you

Days and nights I was lonely and longing for your sex

Craving for your sweet melodramatic voice pumping in my

ear

But your gave it to your sweet bitches

On Tuesday morning you wrote me a letter saying you

missed me and

Was coming to England

But you never did

But you could of at least

blew me a kiss.

Just try

You have to believe that everything will

Be alright you have to tell yourself you'll live and nothing

Should break you I know it's hard

But just try because you'll see that what I am saying is not

    a lie

And you won't deny my forsaken glory

I want to help you but you have to believe that

Its going to be ok you'll live and it shouldn't break you

The leaves on the trees may start to deteriorate and fall of
But that doesn't mean the world has ended

You have to feel the happiness within you and ignore the
    sorrow that awaits you

I know it's hard but just try

Dreams

They are magical but yet deceiving

They tell you one thing than do another

They hold on to your faith like a desperate child

And then they do something else

That's out of the ordinary

There dreams

They lie to you and deceive you

They say one thing then they do something else

That's NOT RECTIFIED

THEY HURT ME BECAUSE they lie and then they feel

  your head

With foolish clouds

I hate it because what they do is not rectified

They tell you one thing then it's another

These are called our dreams

The queen of England

I wrote this letter and sent it in the post

The day I saw the royal family they looked so beautiful and
    magnificent

In there clothes it's the way they stood that made me smile

They sure where proud of Our England

The way they bestowed such supremacy and honour they
    made me weak but I did not

Dispute cos I new it was rude

The queen of England

Was there she leered at me and respected me

She told me how sweet England

Respected the proud ones

She gave me hope she was the on who helped us

The day that was dull and dead she was the one who shone
through us
And that unfortunate day was here

The queen of England
Sent us food and water when they wasn't any
She smiled at me and told me I was a proud one
And that I mustn't be a loud one
Because it created the wrong attention

Her hat was bent and crooked and spun to one side she
told me
I should wear my hat like hers and not my heart on my
sleeve
She told me shell help us and would send out the proud
ones to support us
But all I say is the queen of England saved us.

Golden light

The light that shone was so luminous so

Beautiful it made the entire room

Feel like it was mine it was exquisite so linguistic it spoke

   without logic

When you walked into the room there was a golden light

It definitely felt like paradise

A spacious place it was, not one part of filtrate or dirtiness

It made me develop an everlasting gaze as I gawked into

   the room

So bravura it brought painful tears of happiness into my eye

This was my room and only mine

Exactly what I had always dreamed of

A golden delight

The path that led into the darkness and through to the

brightness

Was my room and only mine

As the night had darkened the stars fell back into the sky

And the sun came out

And created such a glorious shine through out

My territory

Oh what a delight

It was my golden light

I did everything in there from reading books to sleeping in

there

But I never let anyone in there

As it was my golden delight and I did not want

To spoil it

My golden delight, my golden delight

Even the chairs in the room opened up their arms like a

butterfly

And the floorboards would never squeak and that's exactly

what I liked

It welcomed me to where I belonged

Because it was my darling

My everlasting

My golden delight

Searching

Searching for happiness searching for joy

There it was right there beside me

The daylight was there and the smiles of innocent children

Walking past me

But bitter sweetness of my neighbourhood left tears in my
eyes

Because it was once a jovial place and now it's become
numb at this moment in time

Searching for a bellow of joy but found just a little

Searching for a reason to live and the their it was looking

me dead in the eye

Making me know that I was someone special

Counting my blessings and dismissing the disappointments

Looking for an answer and there it was all along the

answer was you

You gave me the hope that I needed to believe in me

And after all I discovered that I was searching for nothing

because I already had you

Baby baby

Baby please don't leave

I didn't mean to say the things I said

I love you baby and cant live without you

So please don't go cos I no my heart will break real slow

When I told you to fuck of it meant for you to stay

When I lied and said I was coming home I didn't mean to
     do what I did

Baby baby please don't go

Cos my heart will break real slow

Your harmony and breath you breathe is what makes me
     strong

So please don't go cos my heart will break real slow

When you told me you had enough and was leaving

I felt my whole body quiver so violently like an aggressive
    wild animal

You cut my legs and arms when you left

You ripped my sole and then you tor the whole of my heart
    out when you shut that

Fucking door

But my arms and legs and the whole of my body parts are
    back together again

As you came back home and back to me

So baby, baby please don't ever leave me again

Cos what I said was wrong of me

But when you left you spat my heart out and threw it in my

    face

And I can never forget that day

Although you deceived me so I'd never think of leaving you

You cheated and told your friends you didn't love me

So Baby baby please don't leave

Didn't Hurt You

Scurring through the soundless, solitaire street

Needing to get my head straight and obliterate my

Hallucination. I couldn't speak for a moment but thoughts

Bleeding, heart aching words beat my head black and blue

Till I said nothing I dared not to look at you

I felt a fool .I was in a mind of denial and hurt

A hurt that clung to your shoulder and did not let go

It was yesterday I felt that shoulder pulling me down

It poked, pinched mocked me and played with my

   emotions

As if I was clay .they thought I was clay but that didn't

   bother me

You told them this and that; you made every word out of

   nothing, nothing

You said I trapped you, impaired you that bad that it put
     you to the ground

You say a lot but I didn't hurt you. I didn't hurt you when
     telling the truth would evoke such a good outcome on
     you usually

But it did not this time, my pretentious darling you were a
     flower that spoiled with too much attention that got to
     your poor little head

Love me like you used to, be candour to whoever you may
     fornicate with but there would never be another me
     even when you replace me. You'll close your eyes and
     realise

I didn't hurt you but yet you still continue to tell them that

I didn't hurt you

But you still continue to tell me I did

Happy Birthday

Smile for me sweetheart

Please do it for me I know you don't want to

Because you have in your mind that nobody cared about

    the other ones

And the truth is we did

Why does this day cause you to weep terribly?

With pain so painful it aches your innocent heart .It

    makes us feel embarrassingly guilty. The other ones are

    reminiscent over you.

You won't forget.

No matter how much things we get you,

You still won't stop thinking about it. Please try. It

    swallows us up like a hungry wagon.

And you know it.

We brought flowers for you, you always loved flowers

Deep down this day lengthened itself. It didn't want to

come

You didn't want it to

I am trying to make up for those damaging years of lost

love but you won't allow us. Please give us a chance

every day we are sorry, we try but what else can we do?

Today is the day we acknowledged your importance it

is late but is now discovered .absolve our bitter mistake

and take us back into your heart

You need to think amorously about yourself this is your

day and no one else's so smile for yourself but not for

us ,once a pun a time we gave you nothing but we

now trying to make you feel gaspingly special .give us

a chance its killing us beautifully but gradually at the

same time. I don't blame it.

You have lived this long live another one and another one

    you are young bright and a charming child. You deserve

    the best forget about us maybe discard us. No blues, no

    sorrow, no distresses Stop the crying the candles are hot

    and the cake is here.

So blow your nose and let us prepare the table

Happy birthday my dear darling.